TALES OF THE BLACK JACK FOREST

Mary E. Abernathy

ATHENA PRESS.
MIAMI LONDON

TALES OF THE BLACK JACK FOREST
Copyright © Mary E. Abernathy 2002

All Rights Reserved

ISBN 1 930493 61 4

First Published 2002 by
ATHENA PRESS PUBLISHING CO.
1001 Brickell Bay Drive, Suite 2202
Miami, Florida 33131

Printed for Athena Press.

TALES OF THE BLACK
JACK FOREST

Dedicated to Joshua, Jedidiah, Jessica, Lucas,
Hannah and Hope

About the Author

Mary lives with her husband, Charlie, on 160 acres outside Waurika, Oklahoma. Her house sits on a hill overlooking forty acres of woodland. Born in Iowa, she has lived in and around Waurika for some fifty years. She is a retired L.P.N., works as a secretary at the First United Methodist church, and is involved in the rehabilitation of injured or abandoned wildlife. Mary has taken care of deer, bobcats, possums, raccoons, squirrels, rabbits and all kinds of birds, and she and Charlie have numerous pets around their house.

Mary's proudest accomplishments are her son, three daughters, one stepson, three grandsons, two granddaughters and one great-granddaughter.

Contents

Miss Bobby Tail

This happened to me yesterday and I've just been dying to tell someone. As you can see, I live in a beautiful forest of black jack trees, in a place called Oklahoma. Have you ever been to Oklahoma? Well, you must go there someday. Oh, I'm so sorry, forgive me, I was telling you about my experience yesterday.

It was in the early afternoon and I was sleeping so soundly. We raccoons, like most wild animals, sleep in the daytime and do our grocery shopping at night. Well, I was sleeping so soundly, when I was awakened by a noise that I didn't recognize. It was a little cry that sounded like a kitten, but then again it could have been a sick puppy. I peeked out of my hollow log, very carefully because I was scared, and lo and behold, right there at the opening of my log was the cutest little kitten. She was sort of gray with little black spots all over her tummy and the shortest little tail, and she was crying so very hard.

'Little kitten, why are you crying? What is the matter?

Can I help you?' I asked quietly.

'I beg your pardon!' she growled back at me, 'I'm not a little kitten, I'm a ferocious bobcat and my name is Miss Bobby Tail and I'm, I'm, oh boo hoo hoo, I'm so very hungry and I've lost my mommy. Will you help me, please?' cried the kitten. She looked up at me with her big yellow eyes, then she said, 'Say, what are you anyway? You can't be a bobcat – we don't wear funny-looking masks over our eyes and your tail is so long and ugly. My tail is short, like it's supposed to be. Don't you think short tails are cuter?' asked Miss Bobby Tail.

'I beg your pardon, Miss Bobby. You don't need to be so hateful. To answer your questions, I don't have on a mask. This is the way all raccoons look, and as for my tail, *I* think it's just right. If anyone's tail is ugly, it might be yours! If you're going to have a tail, you might as well have a long one!' I told her. 'Please, I'm sorry, please don't cry, I didn't mean to hurt your feelings. I'll see what I can do to help you, if you'll tell me the whole story. Then we will find you something to eat and go to look for your mother. I'm sure she's probably searching for you everywhere,' I tried to console her.

'All right, I'll try,' sobbed Miss Bobby. 'My mother and brother and I live in a very nice apartment underneath the old barn, at the corner of the wood. Mommy had to go out to find us some food and she told Hank, that's my brother, and me that she would find us a nice fat rat for breakfast, and for us to stay and wait for her to come back. Well, you know how well some boys mind and as soon as she left, Hank followed her and he left me all by myself. Now it's getting late in the day and mommy and Hank aren't home and I'm hungry and I want my mommy!' bellowed the little kitten.

'Now, now don't make such a fuss. I'll share my dinner with you. Follow me down to the pond and I'll catch us some nice fish, and I know where the very best berries are growing. Why, you'll be full in no time,' I said.

I led her to our big pond and there, in record time, I'd caught the nicest fish. I washed the fish and then my hands – we raccoons are very clean and we always wash before our meals. I took the fish over to her and, would you believe, she took one look at the fish, smelled it, and then shoved it with her paw and said, 'What is that thing? You don't expect me to eat that, do you? It smells bad and it's slimy and, well, wherever did you get it?' she asked, none too nicely.

'That thing is called a fish, and it feels funny because it is wet. It came out of the water in the pond,' I answered.

'Water? What is water?'

'Water is what you drink and what we use when we take baths.'

'Baths, what are baths?'

'Why, you poor dear! Come over here to the water's edge and I'll show you how to take a bath.'

'Stop, no, stop! Mrs. Raccoon please stop! I don't like that water! I might want to drink it but I don't ever want to get in it. That's just awful,' sputtered Miss Bobby.

'All right, don't panic, you're acting just like a regular ole house cat. I can't believe you don't like to bathe, that's not very nice. Oh please don't start crying again! Just eat your berries and forget about the fish and the water,' I pleaded, 'and please call me Hazel.'

'Oh, Hazel, I'm so sorry but I don't like the berries either. What I need is a big fat rat,' whined Bobby.

'Miss Bobby, I don't know how to get you a rat. I don't even know where rats live or how to catch them, but we'll ask Irving Beaver if he knows what to do. He lives in this pond and he builds dams for a living. He's really very smart and he just might know where we can find a fat rat and how to catch one. Oh, Mr. Beaver, Mr. Beaver, where are you? Please come out,' I shouted.

'Oh, there you are. Excuse me Irving, I'd like you to meet Miss Bobby Tail. She lives under the old barn in the corner of the forest and she has a problem that we thought you might help us to solve.'

'Why certainly I'll be glad to help, just tell me where you want your dam built,' shouted Mr. Beaver.

'No Irving, that's not the problem. Miss Bobby has gotten separated from her mother and brother, and she's hungry. I tried to share my meal with her but she doesn't like fish or berries. She wants a fat rat. Can you tell us where we might find a rat and how we should catch it?'

'What do I look like? The Yellow Pages? I don't happen to associate with rats, fat or skinny! Oh good grief! Tell her to stop that infernal crying! I'll see what *I* can do. Now let me see, who can help us? You see beavers only eat young trees, my favorite is the willow, and I would be more than glad to share it with you. We can go over to the house and I'll introduce you to my wife. I know she'd love to meet you,' offered Mr. Beaver.

'Okay, where is your house?' asked Bobby.

'In the dam at the edge of the pond by the water,' said Irving.

'Water? By water? You've got to be kidding. I'm never going in that stuff again. Besides, how do you think I'm going to eat a tree?' shouted Bobby.

'You know, Miss Bobby, you may be right. Your gnawing teeth are too far apart and they don't stick out just right. Now look at my teeth, they're just perfect for chewing trees. You'd never get enough to eat with those fangs. Wonder why they're so far apart? I'm sorry, Hazel, but I'm afraid I can be of no help to you or Bobby. You might ask Mrs. Daisy Deer, I'll bet she can help you. She lives farther into the woods and she might have seen a fat rat or, better still, she might know where Bobby's mother and brother are at this time.'

'All right, Irving, we'll try to find Daisy. Thank you for your help,' I said.

'Help, what help? He wanted to put me in the water and feed me trees and did you get a look at his tail? Why, I've never seen anything so ugly – it almost looked like a paddle. Who is this Daisy Deer? I'll bet she's just another dumb old animal and she'll probably want to feed me something dumb like grass. Do you really think she can help me?' asked Bobby.

'I certainly hope so, Bobby. You really need help, but I think you need more help with the way you look at other animals, than help finding your mother,' I told her.

'What do you mean, Hazel? Am I looking cross-eyed or something? I look at animals just like you do.'

'No, Bobby, you don't. You seem to be more concerned with the length and appearance of everyone's tail, than with the fact that all these animals are trying to help you. We've offered you our food and shelter and all you can do is criticize. Don't you know God made us all different for a reason, even the way our tails look?' I asked her. 'Do you realize how you hurt animals' feelings with your rude comments?'

'Oh my, Mrs. Raccoon, I'm so sorry. I didn't mean to hurt anyone's feelings. I've just never seen animals that look different from me, or that eat different foods. I guess I have been pretty rude. Please, will you still help me?' cried Bobby.

'Well, of course I will. Just mind your manners, especially around Mrs. Deer. She's very shy and quiet, strangers make her somewhat nervous. Oh, look! There she is now and there she goes, running to hide. Wait, Daisy, wait! It's just ole Hazel Raccoon. I need to talk with you. Please come out, I have a friend here who needs your help.'

'Why, hello Hazel, I'm sorry I didn't recognize you. Who's your little friend? Forgive me, but she looks awfully like a bobcat and you know how afraid I am of bobcats!' said Daisy.

'Oh, Daisy my dear deer, you're afraid of everyone! She looks like a bobcat because she is a bobcat. Her name is Miss Bobby Tail but she is just a baby who has lost her mother and brother, and she's afraid and hungry. Now you have no reason to be afraid of her; she needs your help,' I explained.

'Oh, please forget what I said. I didn't mean to be rude, but you must promise me, that when she grows up to be a big cat you don't bring her back here. You know what a grown bobcat can do to a deer if it is hungry enough,' whispered Daisy.

'Well, of course, I know and you know, but she's too young to know. I'm not out of my head – raccoons don't get along very well with grown bobcats either. The problem is her mother and brother left her alone while they went hunting. Forgive me Daisy, I didn't mean to use that word, I know how upset the word "hunting" makes you. I'll just say her family went to get groceries and they haven't returned and she's afraid and hungry. She wants a fat rat to eat, but I don't know where to get one for her and Irving Beaver suggested we come talk to you,' I explained.

'Gracious, I don't have any idea about the whereabouts of rats, but my two fawns are out in the clearing right now, eating their supper, and she is more than welcome to join them. Come, I'll introduce you to them. You'll have to excuse them, they do seem to be a little shy with strangers at first,' invited Daisy. 'Come here Violet, come Pansy. We have company for dinner. Now don't be shy and do mind your manners. This is Miss Bobby Tail and she is lost and hungry. We have no reason to be afraid of her today. She's just a baby like you two girls and we must be nice to her,' instructed Daisy.

'Hello Miss Bobby Tail, we're pleased to meet you,' the girls said as they came close to the kitten. 'Won't you join us for supper?'

'That's nice girls. There you go, Miss Bobby. Just help yourself – there's plenty for everyone,' coaxed Daisy.

'Yes mam, thank you, I will. I'm so very hungry. Where is it?'

'There Bobby, right in front of you.'

'Uh, all I see is sunflowers and some red and blue flowers and green grass. Please don't tell me that's your dinner,' said Bobby.

'Of course it is. The red flowers are called Indian Paintbrushes and the blue ones are Texas Bluebonnets. You are very fortunate to have them for dessert, but first you must eat your grass. Your mother wouldn't want you fill up on just flowers. Now help yourself,' urged Daisy.

'Thank you very much. I hope you won't think ungrateful, but I can't eat grass and flowers. I have to have meat and I need a fat rat. If you'll just please tell me where to find one or tell me where to find my mom, she'll have one for me. Boo hoo hoo,' cried Bobby.

'Do you see my problem, Daisy? If I don't hurry and find her mother or find her some kind of a rat, I'm afraid she'll turn into a fraidy cat,' I said.

'Yes, that could be a problem, but I don't know how I can be of any help. Maybe you should go ask Clarence Owl. He's the wisest one I know in this forest.'

'Owl! You can't take me to an owl!' yelled Bobby. 'My Mommy told me always to hide from owls. Don't you know owls and hawks can pick up little bobcats and take them back to their nests?' asked Bobby excitedly.

'Yes, my dear, I'm sorry, I wasn't thinking. We won't talk to the owl. I'm sorry, so sorry, it'll be all right. The only thing that I can think of to do now, is go back your apartment and see if your mom has returned home,' I consoled.

'I sure hope she has. I don't mean to hurt your feelings because you sure have been so very good to me, but I sure do want to see my Mommy. Can we go back now?' asked Bobby.

'I don't think that will be necessary. Look over there, by that broken tree. Who is that, Miss Bobby Tail?' I asked.

'Mommy, oh Mommy! Here, look over here! I'm over here! Oh, Mommy I'm so glad to see you. Where have you been?' shouted Bobby.

'Where have I been? Where have you been? Didn't I tell you to stay in your bed until we got back from hunting? I've been so worried about you. Thank the good Lord you're all right. Come with me, your supper is getting cold and I have a nice fat rat for you,' scolded Mrs. Bobcat.

'Gee, mommy, that's just what I wanted. Look, Hazel, a fat rat.

'Hazel? Hazel? Mommy where did Hazel go? She was right here. Hazel where are you?' yelled Bobby.

'Hazel who, my dear? There's no one here but the two of us.'

'Hazel is my new friend. She's a raccoon and she has the most beautiful black mask and her tail is so long and pretty and she introduced me to some of the nicest animals and she is my very best friend, and where could she have gone?' cried Bobby.

'I imagine she felt it would be best if she went on to her home at this time, but I'm sure she knows that you and I are both grateful for her help. Now come and let's go home. We still have a little daylight left and I really need some sleep. I've been up all day looking for you.'

I was hiding while I watched them leave for their home. You see I'm afraid of grown bobcats myself, but I was glad I could help the little kitten. So children, that's how I spent yesterday and I still can't believe I made friends with a bobcat, but I guess you can find good in everyone if you'll only try. Won't you come and visit me again? I'd like to introduce you to all the wild animals that live in Oklahoma, or at least the ones that live in my neck of the woods. I have ever so many stories to tell you.

'Yawl come back now, you hear?'

The Story Of Hazel Raccoon And Family

Hi, I'm so glad you stopped by to hear another one of my stories. The last time I talked with you I didn't have the time to introduce you to my family, so today I thought I'd tell you something about us, Hazel Raccoon and family.

As you already know, we live in the Black Jack Forest outside a small town in Southern Oklahoma. We own a two-bedroom hollow log in the middle of one of the oldest trees in the forest.

I have two children, a boy Lester, and a girl Lois. Lester, my oldest, has the longest nose and the prettiest fluffy tail, while Lois has the darkest black mask on her face. They're both just your typical plump and sometimes 'nosy' raccoons.

Their father Royce, God rest his soul, was trying to cross the highway several months ago and he forgot to look both ways, so now it's just the children and me. But let me get on with my story.

One warm summer evening, just as the stars were beginning to peek out of the sky, Lester decided he wanted to take a walk through the forest, while I was fishing for our supper. Normally I don't like the children to be out in the forest by themselves, but it was such a pretty night, and Lester is getting old enough to have some responsibility – or so I thought. Lois, like most little sisters would, begged to go with Lester, and like most big brothers, Lester didn't want her following after him. So, as their mother, I had to insist he take her with him and, as all good mothers must do, I gave them the usual list of do's and don'ts:

Don't go near the highway!

Don't go across the road to the farmhouse (people and dogs live there and they are a real danger to us).

Don't eat anything without washing it first.

Do take care of each other!

'Do you understand?' I asked both of them. 'Now remember to meet me at the pond when the moon is directly over the abandoned barn and I mean no later! I will have supper ready for you.'

After saying this, we started off in different directions. Now you would think those were good enough instructions, wouldn't you? But, no sooner than they had gotten out of my sight the fussing started.

'Come on Lois, Momma told you to stay with me,' ordered Lester.

'No, you walk too fast. Anyway, you're not my boss, and I want to go that way,' answered Lois, walking off in the opposite direction.

'We can't go that way, that's where the farmhouse is. Besides I want to go visit the deer twins,' argued Lester.

'Go where you want, I'm going over there. I can see some big apple trees and over by the shed looks like a big plump

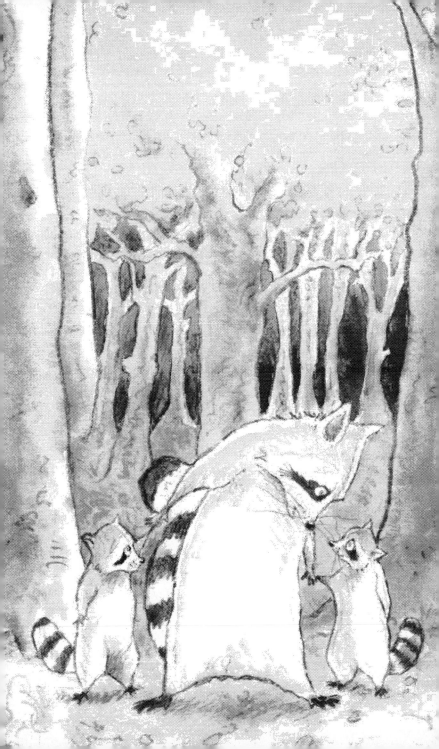

watermelon. We could even go in the shed and look around. There might be all kinds of neat things in there to eat! Come on Lester, don't be a fraidy cat!' coaxed Lois.

'I'm not afraid! It's just that momma said to stay away from the farm, and we'd better do what she said or we'll get in bad trouble,' reasoned Lester.

'Oh Lester, she'll never know and we might even find some nice apples to take to her to have with our supper. Then she'll be really proud of us.'

'Well – I don't know…'

'All right, Mr. I Don't Know, while you're thinking about it, I'm going over there to see what I can find and I'm not going to share it with you. So there,' pouted Lois.

It really is hard to be good when someone else keeps trying to get you to do something you know you shouldn't, isn't it? Well, that's the problem Lester is having right now. What Lois wants to do sounds like so much fun, but then again their momma has told them not to do that. I wonder what Lester will do?

'Oh, all right, I'm coming. I don't know why I'm coming, but I'm coming' shouted Lester. 'Look Lois, there's some nice shiny apples on that tree. Let's get some of them and go back,' he suggested.

'No! I want to see what's in that shed. I'll bet there's some neat stuff in there.'

'No Lois, no! Oh good gravy, now she's in the shed. What was that awful noise? Oh gee, I'd better go in and see about her. Why couldn't I have had a big brother instead of a little sister? Lois, where are you? Oh no! What happened to you? What is that red sticky stuff on you? Are you all right? Talk to me, Lois!'

'Hush, Lester, I'm okay. I just knocked over these cans and they're full of this red stuff. What does it say it is, on the can?' asked Lois.

'Well, how would I know? You know raccoons can't read! I sure wish we could at times like this. Now what are you doing?' asked Lester.

'This green stuff, it looks good, wonder what it is? I'm going to taste it. Do you want some of it?' asked Lois.

'Don't do that, Lois, it says on the sack that it's poison!'

'Now you just said you can't read, will you make up your mind?'

'I can't read, but everybody knows that a picture with a skull and crossbones means that whatever is inside is poison. Don't you know anything?'

'Gosh, Lester you're right! You just saved my life. I wish I didn't have this red stuff all over me. Everywhere I step I leave red footprints. Golly, I sure do seem to be making a big mess. What should I do?' asked Lois.

'Right now be quiet, I think I hear—'

'Hear what, Lester? What do you hear?'

'Quick, Lois, come on! I hear the farmer and his dog! Run for your life!'

'Oh Lester, there's two of us, we can whip that ole dog.'

'No we can't Lois, that's a coon dog and they're trained to catch raccoons. Hurry, run up that tree, hurry!'

'Good dog, Blue. Let's see what you've got up that thar tree. Why it's nothin' but a couple of baby coons and one of them must be hurt, looks like it's got red blood all over it. Ain't no sense in messing with them. Not much sport in catching an injured baby coon. Let's go on back to the house, I only hunt for the big ones,' said the farmer.

'Oh, thank the Lord, Lois, we're saved. Come on and get down. Let's get to the pond as quickly as we can. Boy, is momma going to be mad. Why did I ever listen to you?'

'Uh-uh, mommy won't be mad at me. I'm injured and covered with blood and you were supposed to take care of me,' pouted Lois.

'Aw Lois, hurry up. I'm not going to be late too, we're already in enough trouble.'

'I know, you shouldn't have let me go over to that farmhouse. I could have really been hurt, and you're the oldest and you promised mommy you'd take good care of me. Aren't you ashamed?' asked Lois.

Well, can you imagine my shock, when I looked up and saw my two babies running over the hill. Lois looked like she'd had a bath in red paint. 'What on earth has happened to you?' I asked.

'Oh mommy, don't be mad. I'm injured and a dog chased us and the man said he didn't want a coon that was covered in blood and—'

'Covered in blood, Lois raccoon? You're not hurt anywhere, you're covered in red paint, but you may hurt when I get through with you,' I said.

'Don't be mad at Lois, momma, it was all my fault. I'm the oldest and I should have minded what you said. Punish me,' said Lester.

'No, no, mommy. Lester saved my life. He wouldn't let me eat the green stuff that was poison and he told me not to go to that farm in the first place and I didn't mind him, so punish me,' cried Lois.

'It seems to me that the scare you both have had is punishment enough for now, but in the future, you should remember that mommies only make rules to keep their children from harm. Will you remember that?' I asked my little ones.

'Yes, oh yes, we'll always remember,' they said.

'Do you think they will remember? Neither do I.'

The Town That Wasn't
And The Dog That Isn't

Hey, boys and girls! My name is Buford Bluejay and I live in a tree close to Hazel Raccoon, and I wanted to tell this story. Some people say I'm nosy and pushy, but let me tell you that's not always true. Sometimes I am very quiet and would never, ever gossip, but I've just got to tell you this one story, 'cause I know it's true.

A month ago I was flying around the county. Our county is named after a president, it's called Jefferson. Do you know the name of your county? What? Oh yes, I am sorry, I forgot, I was telling you a story. Well, I overheard some big people talking about a town in Lawton, Oklahoma that was getting way too big and they were going to have to move the whole town! But that's not all they said, now listen to this, the town is made up completely of dogs! Yes, dogs! No, I understood exactly what they said. A whole town full of dogs is going to have to be moved, they said. Either they moved the town or they would have to put them to sleep, and you know what that means!

I hurried as fast as I could back to my little forest to tell Clarence Owl the news. I was so excited, but all he did was wink at me, turn his head and then he said, 'Oh yes, I know all about that. I've been expecting them for several weeks now.'

'You mean a town is moving here? Why, that's awful, what will we do? A town full of dogs, at least it's not cats, but oh, no!' I screeched.

'Buford, calm down. It's not as bad as you think, only some of them are actually moving here,' soothed the Owl. 'I'll tell you what, you tell all the animals in the forest to meet me tomorrow at three o'clock in the afternoon at the old abandoned barn and they'll get to see the new town and meet their leader. Tell them not to worry. They are very nice little animals and the new town will not be in the forest. They want to be on flat land and they don't like trees,' said the owl.

'You know their leader?' I asked. 'What is he like? Will they hurt us? Oh, why do they have to move here?'

'Mr. Bluejay, will you get ahold of yourself? You're getting all excited about something you don't understand and you are judging a whole town that you've never even met. That's not very nice or very smart of you,' scolded Clarence.

I flew off to tell all the animals in the forest and before I was through delivering my message, my story had gotten quite twisted and wasn't anything like what Clarence had asked me to say.

'Honest Mr. Coyote, it's a whole town moving in here, and they're going to take over and run us out. They said they would catch us while we're asleep and steal all our food and I just can't tell you what else, it's just too awful! Anyway,

Clarence wants us all to meet at the old barn at three o'clock tomorrow afternoon and run them out!' I exaggerated.

'I'm usually fast asleep at that time. But you can count on me to be there. We don't need any giant wild dogs moving into our forest,' growled Clyde Coyote.

It was really hot that afternoon and all the forest creatures were waiting patiently by the barn. If you had driven by in a car, however, you would never have seen them. Each one has his own way of hiding where they can see you but you don't see them and even though they talk like they're big and mean, they're really just little animals who are afraid of all people.

As Clarence Owl flew over the barn, he saw all the animals creeping closer to the road, trying to see the new town and its members.

'Well, what do you think of the new town? It isn't what you thought it would be, is it?' asked Clarence.

'What town? Clarence, did you tell us a story? There isn't any town over there. I don't see even one building! Why, there isn't a town and there are no dogs,' said Hazel, disappointedly.

'No, neither do I and there are no houses either. Clarence, what's going on? Where is the town and the dogs we're supposed to fight?' asked Clyde Coyote.

'If you'll be quiet, I'll introduce you to the top dog right now,' said Clarence. 'Larry Prairie Dog, I'd like you to meet Clyde Coyote. Clyde, please say hello to Larry, the leader of the new prairie-dog town.'

Clyde turned around and there stood a little animal that looked a lot like a ground squirrel with a bobbed tail. Just as Clyde was about to speak, the prairie dog walked over to him

and kissed him right on the forehead.

'What on earth do you think you're doing?' sputtered Clyde.

'I'm sorry,' said Larry, 'but it's our custom. When a strange new dog comes to town, we meet and kiss, then everyone knows we're all friends and they feel free to enter our town. You see we don't fight anyone. We just believe in living peacefully together,' explained Larry.

'Well, how sweet,' giggled Daisy Deer. 'We should all practice that custom.'

'Speak for yourself,' growled Polly Possum. 'How would you like to have to greet George Skunk that way?'

'Aw, Polly, that's not fair,' whined George. 'I don't smell that bad, but I do have a question for you, Mr. Prairie Dog,' said George.

'Why certainly, Mr. Skunk, I'll try to answer all your questions. We should know all about each other if we're going to live so close,' said Larry.

'I'd like to know where your town is. I don't see one, and Clarence said you were moving the whole town into that field. When are you going to start moving?' asked George.

'But Mr. Skunk, the town is already there,' said Larry.

'Where?' asked all the animals. 'We don't see it. All we can see is some dirt.'

'Come on over and I'll show you,' suggested Larry.

'No, no, we can't go out in the open field in the broad daylight!' yelled all the animals.

'That's right, I forgot. Well, let me try to explain our town to you. Everywhere you see a pile of dirt, underneath it is a home. Our streets run from home to home, underneath the ground,' explained Larry.

'You mean your whole town is under the ground?' asked Clyde.

'Sure, it's safer that way. We take turns standing on top of the ground close to our houses and guard each other while we hunt for food. Right now, I'm standing watch for my neighbor while he hunts for food for his family and, after he's found enough food, he will stand guard for me, while I hunt,' explained Larry. 'If one of us doesn't find enough food, the others will share theirs. You see, we try to live like one big family, and if one of us gets sick or hurt, the others will take him into their home and every one of us will take turns taking care of him until he gets well. Or if one of us tries to cross the road and gets hit by a car, the others will go to get him and bring him back to town and we'll bury him.'

'I am so impressed,' said Daisy Deer. 'Clarence, why on earth did you tell us to be afraid of the dogs and say we would have to fight them? You really should be ashamed,' added Daisy.

'That brings up another question. Why do you call yourselves dogs? You don't look anything like me and I'm from the dog family,' asked Clyde Coyote.

'Oh, we're not really dogs at all, we're from the rodent family. You know, rats, mice, squirrels, animals like that. But people named us prairie dogs because we live in the prairie and when we're on guard duty and have to talk to each other, our voices sound like little dogs barking,' said Larry.

'Well, I'll be,' muttered Irving Beaver. 'You should have heard all the stories we heard about you and your town before we met you. We were really afraid of you, but now we can see that you are really very gentle animals and no danger to us at all.'

'I'm afraid we do cause some harm to others, even though we don't mean to do so. Sometimes, because of our holes, we cause cattle to fall and break their legs. They just don't always look where they are going and they will step into one of our holes and fall down. We also love large families and we tend to need more and more land for our town, and that angers the farmers,' admitted Larry.

'Yes, I can see how that could be a big problem,' pondered Clarence.

'I'm just glad we don't have anything to fear from you,' said Hazel Raccoon.

'No, you don't. In fact, we're the ones who'll have to be afraid of you. I just heard Mrs. Bobcat say she'd like to have some of our little dogs for supper tonight, and I don't think she meant inviting them as guests!' answered Larry.

'Oh dear, what will yawl do to protect yourselves, since you don't believe in fighting?' asked Daisy.

'It's simple, Miss Daisy. Most wild animals sleep in the day and hunt at night, isn't that right?' said Larry.

'Yes, of course. Everyone knows that.'

'We sleep safely in our homes at night and we hunt during the day, so we feel pretty safe,' he replied.

'I see,' said Clarence, 'and since this day is almost over, I guess we'll go hunt and let you go to bed. It's really been nice meeting you. By the way, we really are ashamed of how that bad story about you got started.'

'That's all right. We know how easily stories can get started. You all come back and see us now, you hear?'

And with that the prairie dogs went back to live in their town and the forest creatures went back to their homes in the woods and only rarely did they ever see each other again.

So I hope that the next time someone wants to tell you something that's not very nice about another person, you'll remember the story about the prairie dogs and try not to believe everything you hear.

Mr. George Skunk

My name is George, and once upon a time, I guess I was about the unhappiest animal in the forest. You see, I thought I had no friends. No, not even one. I thought that no one liked me, because everyone leaves when I come out to play and no one ever talks to me. Oh, what I would give for just a good old friendly hug! I've thought about this and thought about it but I still don't know why I'm not popular. I'm a little overweight and I tend to waddle when I walk, but other than that, I think I'm pretty cute. I'm black with the neatest, white racing-stripes and I have a little button nose and beautiful brown eyes and I'm fairly smart. I don't eat much and I will clean up all the leftovers people throw out on the roadways, if I get a chance. I just don't know what it is about me that other animals don't like. Okay, all right, I do know why no one wants to be near me. It's because – well – because I stink! There, I've said it.

I don't know why I stink. I'm a clean animal but for some reason every time I get mad or excited and I raise my tail,

everyone runs like crazy, and then I smell it, that awful odor. When I did that it used to make me feel really powerful, because I can make even grown men run from me, but after a while I began to feel very lonesome. Even when I'd try to make new friends and tell them I wouldn't spray them, something might excite me and I really didn't have any control over my spray. I don't think it smells so very bad, do you? My skunk family doesn't even notice it. Did you know that even dogs have an old smelly gland, but theirs doesn't spray? In fact, all animals have a smell about them, that's how they can tell who is who. So why can't they just ignore my smell and be my friend?

I must tell you a funny story about me. I can laugh about it now but at first, I was so embarrassed and then I got mad, and then sad. But now I know it was just funny. If you want, you can sit downwind of me and I'll tell you all about it.

As George started to tell his tale, all the forest animals crept in quietly and took their seats, out of smelling range, and listened to his story.

'It was just at the same time the prairie dogs moved in across the road. They had settled down for the night, so I thought I'd just wander over there and look around the town while everyone was asleep. That way they wouldn't have to take a look at me and run away and hide.

'The night was really pretty, and there was a bright moon shining with the stars twinkling down at me. I guess I was just not thinking about where I was going, because I walked clear through the dog town and right into the settlement of lake homes. I was really scared, because people will shoot skunks that get into their yards, and I started to run back to safety, when I saw her – standing in the lights – the most beautiful skunk I've ever seen. She was standing so very still in the spotlight, right in someone's front yard! She wasn't as big as me, but her stripes were prettier and her eyes were prettier and, well, I just fell head over heels in love!

'The whole time I watched her, she never moved a muscle. I was just fascinated with her, and before I knew it, the sun was starting to come up in the east and I knew I had to get back to my home and sleep, but I hadn't even spoken a word to her. I decided I had to say something to let her know that I wanted to meet her, so as I waddled away I called out to her, "My name is George and I'll be back tonight. If you'd like to, meet me tonight here at the same place."

'I didn't wait for her to answer, I just left, and all day long I couldn't sleep for thinking about her. When I got up I couldn't eat, I was in such a big hurry to get back to the lake. I couldn't believe how brave she was to stand in that yard like that, and she must have stood there for hours. Oh, I hoped she'd be there that night. What would I say to her? What if she's married? What if she's not and she likes me? I was just a bundle of nerves.

'I arrived at the lake houses just after dark and, would you believe it, there she stood, right in the exact same place as last night. She must want to meet me. Oh, I was so happy!

'I called to her to come over, out of the light, to where I was standing, but she just stood there. I thought she must be bashful, so I decided to just talk to her from where I was standing. I told her all about myself, and she never said a word. I thought that was rather odd, so I asked her to tell me about herself. Still not a word, and how could she stand so still? Once again the good old sun was about to catch me, so I told her I would see her again that night. All the way home

I worried about why she wouldn't talk to me or why she wouldn't even tell me her name. Was it because I smell so bad? No, it wouldn't be that, because all skunks smell bad. Maybe she just doesn't like the way I look? No, she and I look alike, so what could it be? I know! I'll bet she's hard of hearing and doesn't want anyone to know. I know what I'll do! I'll do like the prairie dogs do when they meet a new dog. I'll just go right up to her and kiss her on the forehead and then she'll know we're friends. Yes, that's just what I'll do, I thought. Do you see how badly I wanted a friend? Well, that's just exactly what I did! That night, before I lost my nerve, I just waddled over to her and kissed her right on the forehead – and that's when I realized she was only a statue.

'I didn't have time to think about what I'd done, because right then I heard someone yell, "Ma! Fetch me my shotgun, there's a real live skunk in our front yard, and it's standing by that silly ole statue."

'Boy, did these little fat skunk paws run! I ran faster than Crawford Crow can fly. I didn't even slow down until I reached the prairie dog town and that's when I became so embarrassed I could have cried. Imagine, what would have happened if the forest animals had seen that? Why, they would never quit teasing me. They would make fun of me forever! How could I have been so stupid? What a dumb skunk I am. Imagine me, night after night, visiting with a piece of plaster! How embarrassing!

'I went off for several days and just hid. Then one morning, I realized how silly I had been acting and how funny the whole thing really was, and now I can laugh at myself and I don't care if you animals know or do make fun of me!'

At that moment, Hazel Raccoon just walked right up to

George and kissed him on his cute little button nose, then Daisy Deer, Polly Possum, and Irving Beaver did the same.

'What's going on?' asked George.

'Well, you see, George,' said Clyde Coyote, 'we already knew all about your embarrassing situation, but we weren't ever going to say anything about it to you. Clarence Owl was doing some night flying that particular night and he heard you talking to someone, so he flew lower and realized you were talking to the statue. He came back and told us, and the next night, we all followed you. We thought it would be funny, but as we listened to the things you said to her, it made us realize how lonely you must really be.'

'Why didn't you say something? Why didn't you make fun of me? It was funny, wasn't it?' asked George.

'Make fun of you? We would never make fun of a friend, George. It isn't nice to make fun of, or laugh at, someone. You should always make fun with and laugh with your friends. Anyway, we didn't think seeing you so sad was funny,' said Daisy Deer.

'A friend? Did you say a friend?' asked George.

'Why yes, certainly,' answered the animals.

'Does that mean that you are all my friends?'

'Of course we are, George, we always have been.'

'But sometimes you act like you don't like me,' said George.

'Well, sometimes we don't like what you do. Don't you know that you can't like everything about everybody, but if you're friends you just put up with some things? You see, we don't like it when you spray that awful smell. You can always find something about someone that you don't like, but just the same, if you try, you can always find something to like about everyone,' said Clarence Owl, the wisest one in the forest.

'Gee,' said George, 'I'm so happy… I think I'd better go now, I must have something in my eyes.'

It made all the animals in the forest feel kind of sad to see George cry, but they knew that this time his tears were happy tears. He knew that no matter what, he did have friends in the forest.

Clyde Coyote And The Twins

It was a very cold day in late winter. Snow had covered the ground and Clyde Coyote and his wife, Alice, were trying to stay warm and dry in their home in the woods. Clyde had worked very hard during the fall to dig a nice, large hole in the ground, called a burrow. He made sure it was deep enough and big enough to be comfortable for him, Alice and the baby coyote they were expecting in the spring. They spent many winter evenings talking about the new coyote puppy. Clyde was sure it would be a boy, and he bragged a lot about how he would teach him to howl the loudest and the longest of all the coyotes in the forest. Alice would just smile because secretly she hoped it would be a little girl. She could just see herself and the little puppy playing together in the wild flowers that bloomed so brightly every spring. She would teach her to know the different names of all the flowers and where to hunt for the best food for her family. But deep down it didn't matter to either of the coyotes what the puppy was, just as long as it was a healthy, happy puppy. They could hardly wait until spring.

Alice had curled up in a little ball and was almost asleep when Clyde's stomach started to growl. 'Gosh, Alice, I sure hate to leave you alone, but I've just got to go out and get us something to eat,' he said.

'I really wish you'd wait until the morning. It's so cold out there,' said Alice.

'Oh, don't worry about me, I'll be back before you know I'm gone,' and with that Clyde ran out into the snow. Luck was with him and he immediately found a nice fat rabbit to take back to Alice. Won't she be surprised? he thought but the surprise was for Clyde.

He heard some strange noises when he entered the den and, lo and behold, there was Alice with her little girl-puppy, and also with Clyde's little boy-puppy.

'Alice! Twins! You can't be serious, we've got twins? I can't believe what a lucky ole coyote I am.' Then Clyde let out a long and very loud howl to let the whole forest know of his good fortune.

Spring came soon and Clyde took little Roy out with him every day, to teach him everything a young male coyote needs to know. How to run, hunt, hide, but most of all how to sit and howl. But, believe it or not, little Roy couldn't get the hang of howling. He could bark with the best of them but he just couldn't howl. It was really becoming embarrassing to Clyde because he had bragged so much about how his pup would howl the longest and the loudest of them all.

Alice would take little Susie out and try to teach her, but Susie could never remember the names of all the flowers. Now Susie could hunt rabbits as well as Alice and she knew all the best hiding places, but she just didn't have what it took to name all the wild flowers, and besides that she really didn't care. Roy and Susie were clearly very well behaved pups and they were quick to learn everything except howling and flower identification.

One beautiful hot summer morning, Alice and Clyde decided to skip the lesson for the day and take the twins on a picnic. As they were racing across the hills and the meadows, Roy came to a complete stop.

'Oh, look, Dad! Aren't those the prettiest Indian Paintbrushes you ever saw?' he said.

'What are you talking about? I don't see any Paintbrushes,' growled Clyde.

'Why Clyde, he's talking about the wild flowers. Roy, do you know the names of those over there?' asked Alice.

'Sure, those are bluebonnets and those are black-eyed Susies and that's a sunflower and over there are a few primroses,' answered Roy.

'You mean you can name all the flowers?' asked Alice.

'Sure, can't everybody?' asked Roy.

'No sonny, I guess everybody can't, can they Susie?'

Susie looked at her Mother and then she threw back her head, closed her eyes and let out the saddest, longest, loudest howl Clyde had ever heard.

'Well, I'll be!' exclaimed Clyde. 'Can you beat that? God sure showed us a thing or two. I got my boy and you got your girl, and I got my howler and you got your flower-picker, but not the way we planned. I guess that's what we get for trying to say only boys can do a certain thing and girls can only do other things. I guess everyone can be or do whatever their heart tells them to do. What do you say, momma?'

'I say we sure got two neat coyote pups!'

Billy Ben Buffalo The VII

'Daddy, the Countiss's have the funniest-looking old cow in their pasture. You've got to come see it. See, standing there against the fence, a big cow with a little one. I never saw cows that looked like that!' said David excitedly.

'That's because those aren't cows, David, those are buffaloes,' said David's dad.

'A buffalo? You mean a real, live buffalo, like the one on the nickel?' asked David.

'Yes son, you don't see too many of them around any more. They're on the endangered list.'

'What does that mean?' asked David.

'Well, that's when some animals are about to all die out and the government puts them on a list to let everyone know that there's not very many of them left, and that we need to do everything we can to save them. It is against the law to hurt them. You know, you can't buy or sell a buffalo without the permission of the U.S. government,' David's father told him.

'Oh, I hope they don't die out, they're really cool-looking. But that biggest one looks like he has a tear in his eye. Why would a buffalo cry?' wondered David.

'Don't be silly, son. He's not crying, he's just got something in his eye. Come on, we've got to get home for supper.'

★

'Daddy, daddy. Did you see that real live little boy standing over there by the fence?'

'Yes son, I did,' replied William Benjamin Buffalo.

'Why did he ask if you are crying? You are crying, why are you crying?' asked the little bull calf.

'It just makes me so sad, Billy Ben, when humans don't realize how important the buffalo was and that it's really their fault we almost died out. You know humans are cute but sometimes they are really careless.'

'Are you about to tell me a story, daddy?'

'If you want to call it that, I guess I am. Do you want to hear about the Billy Ben Buffalo that had your name first?'

'Oh yes please, daddy. You always said you would tell me when I got older. I guess I'm old enough now, huh, daddy?'

'If you are old enough, Billy, you won't be rude and talk while I'm talking, do you understand?'

'Yes sir,' said Billy as he sat down on the grass to listen to his father's story.

'Many, many years ago your great-grandfather's great-grandfather lived right around here. Instead of Oklahoma, this was called Indian Territory. Old Bill Buffalo the First was wild and free to roam any place he wanted. His only problems were finding enough to eat and drink and hiding

from the Indians,' began William Benjamin Buffalo.

'Why did he have to hide?' asked his son.

'Well son, I reckon the buffalo was just about the most important animal the Indians ever had. They ate our meat, used our hides for clothes, covers and even made tents out of them. They even had a use for our bones. I guess there wasn't a piece of the buffalo the Indians didn't use. I think in some ways it was an honor for the buffalo to give his life so that some young Indian child might have a full belly and a warm hide to sleep in during the cold winters.

'But soon more and more people began to move into Indian Territory. The humans even had a big race on the land, where people lined up and drove their wagons or rode horses or even ran into the land and wherever they ended up, they staked it off and claimed it as their own land. Some people cheated and sneaked in early the night before to get some land to claim. That's how Oklahoma became known as the "Sooner state", because some went in sooner than others. Well, anyway, with all the new people moving in, the buffalo just got in the way, so some people started killing them just for the fun of it. Can you imagine killing just for fun?

'I don't know how ole Bill managed it, but he survived and lived to be an old bull. He married several times and had lots of children before he went to the Happy Hunting Grounds. Every one of our ancestors seemed to be survivors and finally your grandpappy ended up at the Wildlife Refuge in Lawton. You and I were born there, grew up and were just lucky to be sold to this farm. We've really been lucky in lots of ways. One, we're still together and two, we've been bought by really nice people, but we do have a big responsibility, Billy Ben.'

'Like what, dad?'

'We've got to become a part of this herd of cows and raise some calves, that are half-buffalo and half-cattle. They call them Beefalos.'

'Why do they want us to do that?' asked Billy Ben.

'Because the cowboys have finally realized the buffalo has good, lean meat. We're healthy, easy to raise and we make bigger calves, which means more money for our owners.'

'Gosh, dad, I don't know why you were crying, we've got it a lot easier than Grandpa did. We've got lots of food and water and the Indians don't hunt us any more, and it's against the law to hurt us. And, best of all dad, look at this herd of pretty brown-eyed cows just waiting for us to help them raise a herd of little Beefalos. Man, am I proud to be Billy Ben Buffalo the VII.'

Dilly The Dillo

Dilly got up with the sun every morning. He scratched his hard back with his long claws and stretched out his skinny tail. He looked at his reflection in the pond and thought to himself, What a nice long nose I have, and my armor is so shiny, why I'll bet I'm the best-looking armadillo in this part of Oklahoma, probably in all of Oklahoma.

Dilly was an orphan as both his mother and father were killed trying to cross the country road by the Black Jack Forest where they all lived. Dilly had several brothers and sisters but they all went their separate ways when they lost their parents. Dilly had remained in the Black Jack Forest and had become known as the richest creature living there.

One day, while foraging for food in the soft ground near his home, Dilly had unearthed a quarter. He took it home with him and, every night before falling asleep, he would take the quarter out of its hiding place and rub it until it shone. He kept it hidden under his bed of leaves, in some tinfoil he had found. No one was ever allowed to come into

Dilly's home for fear that they might steal his treasure. Dilly, in fact, became really obsessed with his money, and the importance he got from having such a treasure.

Early one cold and rainy morning, Dilly had groomed himself and had just come out of his home, ready for a day of food hunting, when he heard a great commotion at the back of his house. He ran around there just in time to meet Theodore Fieldmouse. Theodore was wet from the rain and although it was cold, he was sweating and shaking at the same time.

'Oh thank goodness, you are still home Dilly. I need to hide in your house for a little while; the big red-tail hawk is after me. He's just behind those trees. I was afraid you wouldn't be home and that he would catch me. I bet I've run a mile from him, hiding under branches and leaves, trying to get here. This was the only safe place I could think of between where I was and home,' panted Theodore.

'What were you doing so far away from home in the first place?' asked Dilly.

'Well, since Brenda and I have had the kids, it gets harder and harder to find enough food to keep them fed. We go off in different directions so that we can bring enough home for the day. You just don't know what it's like feeding a family,' said Theo.

'No I don't and probably never will. I've got better sense than have a passel of brats like you've done. Anyway, I'm afraid you are just going to have to run along and hide some-place else. You know that I have my money hidden in my house and I can't take the chance that you might find it and steal it,' said Dilly.

'Dilly, you can't mean that! Why, if that hawk gets ahold

of me, he'll eat me. You have to help me!' cried Theodore.

'Not so, I don't have to do anything. You're the one who got too far away from home and you're the one the hawk's after. Anyway, that's what you say, but how do I know it's not just a scheme to get me to feel sorry for you and let you in my house, so you can take everything I have and spend it on your family. If I wanted my money to be spent on someone else I would do it myself, but since I don't, I won't, and that's the end of the discussion.'

With that, Dilly walked away, leaving Theodore standing in the cold rain, begging for shelter and protection from the hawk.

Dilly walked on into the woods convincing himself that he had done the right thing. After all, it's a cruel world and everyone in it has to look out for themselves, because nobody else will, thought Dilly. As evening approached Dilly made one last thrust into the dirt with his long nose and out came a nickel. 'Well, that just proves what I thought. If that stupid mouse had spent more time looking for money instead of worrying about the hawk he might have found this nickel and then he wouldn't have to worry about food. He could have just bought some. Of course, with that family hanging on to him the money wouldn't last long. You won't catch me in a mess like that. I'll always have money, and when you have lots of money you don't need family or friends, because all they want is your money anyway. But you can bet they won't get mine,' boasted Dilly, as he started home with his nickel to add to his treasure.

Thirty cents, I'll bet there's not another animal in Oklahoma that has as much money as Dilly Dillo has, thought Dilly as he wrapped the nickel up with his quarter

and tucked them both safely away under his bed. 'Oh, it's nice to be rich. I don't have to worry about anything. I wonder if that dumb field mouse ever made it home to his wife and kiddies, and how he explained to her that he couldn't get any food 'cause a big ole nasty hawk chased him away. Boy, I'll bet he caught it from her and those snot-nosed kids! Am I ever lucky I don't have to answer to anyone about where I go or what I do and all my wealth is mine alone. Boy, am I lucky!' and with that thought Dilly fell asleep, dreaming about finding more money.

The next morning the sun was shining and the day felt warm and lazy to Dilly as he left his home to stroll in the forest. As he topped the hill by the old cow-tank, he came upon Benny Bunny and his wife Rose Rabbit talking to Daisy Deer. As he got nearer to them, he saw Pearl and Paul Possum over by the dam and they were both crying uncontrollably.

'What's going on?' asked Dilly.

'Oh my, haven't you heard the sad, sad news? Theodore Fieldmouse was captured yesterday and killed by the hawk. It happened not far from your house. Poor ole Theo was out looking for food, and when he didn't come home last night, his wife Brenda asked Pearl and me to look for him. It wasn't a pretty sight,' said Paul.

'If only he had made it to your door,' said Daisy, 'he would have been safe inside your house.'

About that time, Bertrum Mouse came out of the grass. 'How are Brenda and the kids doing?' asked Bertrum.

'As well as can be expected at a time like this. Thank the Lord she has friends and family to see her through this, but she is going to need help with the expenses. You know, the burial, and then trying to feed all those baby mice until summer gets here. By then they will be big enough to get their own food, but until then I'm afraid she's going to need all of us to pitch in and help her,' said Daisy.

'I've been living in a tin can I found, but it's really too big for just me, so I'll give that to Brenda and I'll find someplace else to live,' said Alice Mouse.

'Yes, and I have some extra corn I've been saving for a rainy day, but the twins and I really don't need so much to eat. She's welcome to that,' offered Daisy Deer. 'That will really help her, and I know that Dilly has some extra money that he can contribute to the funeral expenses,' suggested Benny Bunny.

'Oh that would be just great, now Brenda won't have to worry about anything!' said Bertrum.

'Wait just a darn minute!' shouted Dilly. 'Dilly Dillo has extra money because he doesn't squander it on anything that comes along. Now, granted I'm sorry that Theo met his match with that hawk, but it isn't my fault and I'm certainly not responsible for his wife and family. That was his problem and now it's hers. Animals should think about things like this before they get married and start raising a bunch of kids. I have my money because I don't have to worry about anyone, and that's the way it's going to stay. So before you start giving away my money you might want to check with me.' And again Dilly walked away from someone in need.

The spring turned into summer and then fall was upon the forest. The days were shorter and the nights were getting cold. Dilly went about his business as usual, but he noticed that even though the forest creatures were never rude to him they were never really friendly to him any more. He tried to convince himself that this didn't matter as long as he still had his treasure, that he didn't need anything or anyone else, but something was missing from his life. The coins just didn't seem to make him happy anymore. Why, he would even forget to shine them every night.

He thought a lot about Theodore and what might have happened if he had gone ahead and let him hide in his house. But then how could he have known that Theodore really was in danger and not just wanting to find Dilly's treasure? Surely no one could really blame him, and Brenda and the mice were doing just fine. He had heard one of the other animals talking about how well they were getting along so no one was really hurt. He just kept trying to convince himself that he had done nothing wrong. Still something kept him from sleeping well at night and it seemed like he always had butterflies in his stomach. Try as hard as he could not to, he did miss having friends.

★

It was a really cold and windy day in the forest and Dilly was hurrying home. His armor didn't hold out the cold and the rain and he was very uncomfortable. The day hadn't been good for root hunting either. As he was running along with his eyes half-closed to keep out the rain, he failed to see the big hole that was holding an old, abandoned concrete septic tank, where an old farmhouse had fallen down and blown away. The tank was at least five feet deep and it was filling with rainwater. Kerplunk! Dilly fell headfirst into the tank. The sides were steep and slick and, try as he might, Dilly could not get a toehold and couldn't climb out. He called and called for help but no one answered him.

The rain finally let up, but Dilly was cold and hungry and, above all, scared. No one will even look for me, thought Dilly. Even if they did miss me they probably will think, good riddance. I have been such a fool and so selfish. What good is my treasure going to do me now? I'd do better if I didn't have any coins but had friends instead, then maybe someone would care enough to come to find me. Dilly cried a little and then he noticed a bright, shining star in the sky and a thought popped into his head. He remembered a story his mother had told him and his brothers and sisters.

It was a long time ago but his mother had said something about a person that lived in the heavens and that he had had a little boy, whom he had sent to Earth to live with the other humans, but that they had killed him. Somehow however, that was all right because the boy had died for everyone's sins so that when we die we might go live with him in heaven. Dilly felt a feeling of peace come over him, and he thought that if this boy had died for Dilly's sins then maybe he had been forgiven for the way he treated Theodore and Brenda, and maybe it wouldn't be so bad to die after all. With this thought Dilly drifted off to sleep but was soon awakened by an awful smell. He rubbed his eyes and looked up to see George Skunk peering down at him.

'Dilly, how in the world did you get in this mess?' shouted George.

'I wasn't looking where I was going and I fell in, and I'm sure cold and hungry,' said Dilly. 'Maybe you have an old blanket you could spare and a root or two? I know you don't want to have anything to do with me, and you sure don't want to help me after all the things I've done to others, but I know I'll die soon in this tank and you are more than welcome to my coins after I'm gone. Maybe you could see your way to share them with Brenda Mouse, and tell her how· sorry I am, if it's not too late. I wish she could find it in her heart to forgive me,' sobbed Dilly.

'You're not making any sense, Dilly. You just keep your chin up and I'll figure out how to get you out of there,' said George. 'Maybe if I can get this tree limb down to the tank you can climb up and out.' George pulled and tugged with all his might and got a good-sized limb over to the tank. He yelled for Dilly to get out of the way as he shoved it over the side. 'Now just climb up that limb and you will be free.'

'I can't, George, I'm just too weak and I've broken my claws trying to climb this wall. It's no good. I'm a goner but I do want to thank you for trying to help, it really means a lot to me. I wish I'd gotten to know you better before this. Shoot, I wish I'd done a lot of things different before this, but now it's too late. I just hope the little boy in heaven died for me too,' cried Dilly.

'Dilly, we'll talk about this after we get you out of there.' With that, George began to shout for help. Immediately, three of Theodore and Brenda's children ran over the hill.

'What's the matter? What's happened?' yelled all three of them at the same time. George took them over to the tank and showed them Dilly and explained the situation.

'Well,' said Petie, the oldest mouse, 'if we ran down the limb and got in the tank with him we could push him up.'

'That's a good idea,' said George, so the three little mice ran down the limb and got behind Dilly and started to push. They pushed and they shoved with all their might but they didn't move Dilly an inch.

'This won't work, we're not strong enough to push him. We'll need someone who is bigger and is good at climbing trees.'

'That lets me out,' said George, 'I can't climb anything, but I do have another idea. You mice stay with Dilly and I'll go see who else I can find to help.' With that, George scurried away, leaving a very unpleasant odor behind.

'Do you really think he will be able to find anyone else willing to help me?' asked Dilly.

'Well, sure, why not? You're a forest creature in need. Everyone will want to help,' said Rosco Mouse.

'I'm not so sure. I've been a really bad armadillo and I doubt that anyone cares what happens to me. I don't understand why you three stopped to help.' Dilly hung his head. 'You know, after all what I did to your family.'

'What do you think you did to our family?' asked Petie.

'Well, first of all when your daddy came to me for help to hide from the hawk, I refused to let him in my house, for fear that he really just wanted to steal my coins, and it's my fault the hawk got him,' Dilly started to cry.

'I don't know who told you that, Dilly. Dad did hide in your house. He stayed there until he knew the hawk had left and then he came on home. It was a couple of hours later that he decided to try his luck again at hunting, and he went back out. He was headed back in the direction of your house when another hawk spotted him, and well, you know the rest. But it certainly wasn't your fault,' explained Roger Mouse.

'Not my fault? He did hide in my house? How could he have done that? I keep my house locked and safe from all intruders. I always have, because of my money, you know.

He couldn't have gotten in my house,' said Dilly.

'Oh yes he could. Anyone can and always have been able to,' Roger went on. 'You see, there is a rotten board in the back of your burrow and all anyone has to do is pull it back and go on into your bedroom. The room where you keep your money hidden under your leaves,' Roger stated frankly. 'Dilly, anyone of us could have gotten your coins a long time ago.'

'Then why didn't somebody steal them? That's a lot of money and I would never have known who got them,' said Dilly.

'Because they are yours, and frankly, we forest animals don't have any use for money. All of us have found coins at different times but we just left them there. You can't eat them, and we don't need clothes or anything else that they could buy so you are welcome to them.'

Before Roger could explain anymore they heard George (or rather smelled him) coming towards the tank. With him was Hazel Raccoon and her two sons, Daisy Deer and her twins, Miss Bobby Tail, Pearl and Paul Possum, Brenda and the rest of her litter, the rabbits and several more of the forest creatures.

'Now we'll have you out of there before you can say jackrabbit! Excuse me Benny Bunny, that's just a saying,' said George.

Everyone peered over the tank as the two raccoon boys scampered down the limb. They both got behind him and Hazel came down to meet him.

'Grab hold of my tail and give it all you've got,' encouraged Hazel.

With several grunts and groans, the trio soon had Dilly

out of the tank and safely on the ground. 'Hurrah!' yelled the animals, 'Hurrah!'

Dilly started to thank all the animals but he was too overcome with tears to make much sense.

'I'll make it up to you, I promise, I'll change my way, starting right now. I didn't know that you liked me at one time just for me. I was so stupid I thought it had to do with my treasure. And sure enough, it was only *my* treasure, no one else thought it was worth anything. From now on, none of my treasures will be here on Earth. I want to give my house to Brenda and the mice and I'll find another one and I want my thirty cents to go towards food and whatever anyone should need. I want to put it in a safe place, but a place where anyone that ever needs it can go and get it immediately. And from now on any coins that I find will also go in that place and be used to buy more food or whatever, for anyone that needs it,' declared Dilly. 'From now, on my friends come first, and I will worship my Maker not my money!'

'Hip, hip, hooray!' shouted all the little animals together. 'Hip, hip, hooray!'

Terry The Terrapin Meets Gerta The Turtle

Well, hello there, boys and girls. Let me introduce myself. I'm Mrs. Agnes Terrapin and I was just about to tell about a problem I've had with my son, Terry.

It was last spring, when the days were becoming longer and warmer and it must have been the April showers that started the whole thing.

I was in the kitchen, baking a fly pie for lunch, when I happened to see a small turtle crawl into our yard. We live by the pond at the edge of the forest and I knew there were a family of turtles living in the pond, but I'd never met them. I went outside to meet the turtle. She said her name was Gerta and that she was ten years old, just the same age as Terry. She also said she was lonely because there were no more turtle families in the pond and the only ones she had to play with were her brothers and sisters. I immediately invited her in for fly pie, and called Terry to come down and meet her. I thought they could have such a great summer together, but boy was I wrong! I introduced them and after lunch they went outdoors to play, but soon Terry came strolling slowly into the house.

'Why, what's the matter? Where is your new playmate?' I asked.

'I don't know and I don't care. I don't like her,' replied Terry.

'Well, Terry, what on earth happened?' I asked.

'Nothing Ma, she's just a dumb ole turtle and I don't like turtles!'

'Don't like them, how can you say that? She's the first turtle you've ever met. You better come up with a better reason than that,' I scolded.

'Aw, when we went outside, I asked her if she'd like to play in the dust and dirt with me and she said, no, she'd rather play in the pond and she wanted me to get in the water with her! Ain't that dumb?'

'Isn't that dumb, not ain't, and what's dumb about that?' I asked.

'Everyone knows that terrapins don't like water and anybody that does is stupid,' growled Terry.

'I can't believe you said that.'

'Well, do you know what else she did, Ma? She asked me if I'd like a snack and I said yeah, I guess. She went out into that dirty water and brought back a fish. A fish, Ma. Yuk, I can't believe anybody eats those slimy, smelly fish. I don't like anybody that eats fish.'

'Terry!'

'Its true, and Ma, turtles aren't near as pretty as terrapins, because they're just one color and their shells are shaped funny and they walk too fast and I'll bet she's mean, 'cause I heard all turtles will snap at you, and if they can get you in their mouths they won't let go until it thunders and that's why I don't like turtles!' explained Terry.

'Oh Terry, how can I explain to you how wrong you are?' I asked. I listened to Terry and I just wanted to cry. 'You see my son, you must learn early in life, and never forget, that God made us all different for a purpose. If no one liked to go in the water, how boring it would be. Why, there would be no boats and no swimmers or fishermen and everyone would be crowded on the shore! Just because we like to do different things, that doesn't make either one of us stupid, and surely you know everyone in the world can't like the same things to eat, or there wouldn't be enough food to go around. Liking different foods doesn't make us right or wrong, it just makes us different. Did you know that the turtles were here on Earth long before any of us, so if anyone looks ugly or different it would have to be us?

'Terry, why would you not like Gerta, just because her shell is a different color and it's shaped different? It's done that way so she can swim in the water and she isn't too easy to see. It's the same with our color and shape, so we can manage better on land. As for Gerta being mean, why, I've heard that ole snapper story too and we both know that's not true. There are some turtles that snap but not all of them. Can't you see that we can't all look and all think alike?'

Terry thought for a minute and then he said, 'Yeah, I guess I see what you mean. We'd look pretty silly if everyone wore the same clothes and ate the same food and talked and walked just alike. Why, we wouldn't be reptiles or animals, we'd be robots! Maybe we should like every creature for what it is and not want it to be just like us. Is that what you mean, Ma?'

'Yes, Terry. I think if you went back outside and asked Gerta to play with you, maybe she could show you fun things to do in the water and you could show her how to have fun playing in the dirt. Now, about her taste in food, how can you know that you don't like something if you've never eaten it?' I asked.

'Gee, Ma, do you think that Gerta might like to go meet the guys? I'd like to show them how neat her shell is and how different it is from ours and maybe we could play hide-and-seek. If we make her "it", it'll be harder for her to find us on land because of our shells. It's really neat how everything is different for a reason, ain't it Ma?'

'Isn't it, Terry. Yes it really is, it really is.'

Well, boys and girls, that's the problem we had. It may not seem like a big problem, but sometimes it can be. The humans have a word for it; it's called prejudice. Now Terry and the guys have included Gerta and her brothers and sisters in their play, and they have been having hours of fun playing and learning new things about each other. It's a shame some boys and girls don't take lessons from Gerta and Terry about how to get along with others. If you ever hear someone say they don't like someone and the reason is because they are different, you might tell them the story of Gerta and Terry, and explain how silly it sounds to say you don't like someone just because they are different from you. After all, maybe it's not them but you that's different.

Harry Tarantula And The New Shoes

It was almost summer and Harry, his wife and forty little tarantulas were just waking from their long winter's rest.

'Get up, Harry, get up, you've got to hurry,' said Tina, Harry's wife.

'Hurry for what? All we've got to do is get all these young 'uns up and out into the world, all on their very own. I'll miss them, but truthfully it will be nice to have the den all to ourselves again,' yawned Harry.

'What are you thinking, Harry Tarantula? You can't send these little spiders out on their own without new shoes!'

'Without what?' sputtered Harry. 'Shoes, shoes, where on God's green Earth did you come up with that idea?' he asked.

'I don't know, it just came to me and it seems like the proper thing to do. Now hurry, you've got to come back with, now let's see, forty little spiders with eight feet each, that's 160 pairs of shoes,' stated Tina.

'Have you lost your mind? Who ever heard of spiders

wearing shoes? Besides, where would I find shoes in the forest, and how am I going to pay for them? You must be nuts!' yelled Harry, not very politely.

'Nevertheless, our children are going out into this world wearing new shoes. You can go out and ask some of your insect friends where they buy their children's shoes,' demanded Tina.

'What insect friends? You know all the insects are afraid of us. Have you forgotten we eat insects? Insects stop and talk to me – I don't think so – no one talks to a tarantula. Everyone is afraid of us, woman, you can't be serious!'

'I'm very serious and you're just wasting time. Now hurry before the little ones wake up and start wanting to go out into the world. Hurry now, Harry, hurry!' ordered Tina.

'Okay, okay. Boy, oh boy, that woman can be so bossy,' thought Harry.

Now let me see, where should I go first and who will talk to me? Oh well, you never know until you try. I think I'll go over to the plum thicket and have a talk with Ed Caterpillar. If anyone knows about feet and shoes it should be good ole Ed, he thought.

'Good morning Ed. No, no don't run away. Don't be afraid. I just want to ask you a question. Do you know where I can buy some new shoes for my little spiders? The wife is determined to send them out into the world wearing new shoes. Can you help me?' asked Harry. 'Where do you get your children's shoes?'

'I'm sure I don't know Mr. Tarantula, I'm just a teenager myself. I'm just going into my cocoon and I don't even know what shoes are. When I go out into the world on my own, I'll go out as a beautiful butterfly and I won't need anything

called shoes. You'd better ask someone else; maybe they'll know but I sure don't and frankly it's making me very nervous talking to you,' stammered Ed as he walked quickly away.

'Sure, thanks anyway,' said Harry. 'Now, who else can I ask? I've got to find out and get some shoes or Tina will really be mad. I know, I'll ask Mrs. June Bug.'

'Oh, June, June don't be afraid, I need to ask you something. Where do you buy your children's shoes? I've got to buy 160 pairs of shoes for the little spiders and I don't know where to go. Can you help me?' asked Harry.

'I'll try to help you, but I don't even like looking at you. You scare me so. If you don't mind, I'd like it better if you'd face the other way while you're talking to me,' said June Bug.

'Like this?'

'Yes, that's much better, I feel much safer. Now about the shoes. I can't tell you anything about shoes. I just came into this world myself, you see. Before I became a June bug I was a grub worm, and we didn't wear shoes. You might ask the big ole red ant. She's always going here and there and she might know more about shoes. I'm sorry, I can't help you, but I really wish you would go away now.'

'Sure, I understand, but hey, thanks anyway,' Harry called to June as she scuffled away.

Guess I'll just go over to that hill and see if the red ant is home, thought Harry.

'Hey Mrs. Ant, I'd like to ask you a question if you don't mind,' said Harry.

'I don't mind, but you'll have to walk along with me as you talk. I don't have time to just sit and visit. I've lots of work, work, work to do. Now come along, what is it you'd like to know? Please watch where you're going, you're messing up my tracks,' said Mrs. Ant.

'Oh, sorry. I'd just like to know where you buy your children's shoes?' apologized Harry.

'Shoes? I don't buy shoes! I don't have time to buy anything, I have to work. Oh dear, someone missed that crumb over there. Oscar, get that crumb lying over there! Goodness, there's a stick in our way. Come here Frank, Howard, help me move this stick,' she said.

'Now why aren't you working? Who hired you anyway?' asked Mrs. Ant.

'I don't work here Mrs. Ant, I just was asking you about shoes. Remember?' said Harry.

'Oh, yes, well I'm sorry, I don't have any shoes for you. Now will you please run along. We've got work to do today! After all, today is no picnic!'

Golly, what am I going to do? Who can I ask now? Maybe one of those flies over there can tell me, thought Harry. He walked slowly over to the trees where a group of horseflies were practicing their landings.

'Excuse me,' said Harry, 'please don't fly away, I'd like to ask you a question.'

'We're not going to fly away but we're not coming any closer than this to you,' said the lead fly. 'Now, what was it you wanted to know?'

'Where do you buy your children's shoes?' asked Harry.

'Why, flies don't wear shoes! How do you think we could fly if our feet were weighted down with shoes? I never heard of such a thing. I know, this is *Candid Camera* isn't it?' laughed the fly.

'No, no, my wife sent me out to buy shoes for the kids

71

and I don't know where to go,' said Harry.

'Well, I'm sorry but we can't help you. I still think this is a joke,' said the fly as he flew away.

Harry sat down beside a rock and was about to cry when he heard the gentlest voice.

'Pardon me, Mr. Tarantula, but I couldn't help but overhear your conversation with Hoss, the fly, and I thought maybe I could help you.'

Harry looked up into the softest brown eyes he'd ever seen. Daisy Deer was standing over him, her head bowed down, so she could look him in the eyes. 'I've been trying to think of someone who wears shoes, but the only ones I know are my cousins, the horses, and of course the humans. Why don't you go ask the wisest one in the forest, maybe he could help you? If anyone would know, it will be Clarence Owl,' suggested Daisy.

'An owl! Don't you know owls eat spiders?'

'Yes Harry, I know, but if you go talk to him in the daytime he'll be too sleepy to be hungry. You see, owls hunt all night and sleep during the day, but if you hurry you might just catch him before he goes to bed.'

'Thank you, Daisy, and may I ask you one more question? Why aren't you afraid of me?' asked Harry.

'Because I'm bigger than you and if you bothered me I'd just step on you. The thought of you crawling on me gives me goosebumps, but no, I'm not afraid of you,' answered Daisy.

'Thank you, Daisy, I think.'

Harry walked on to the tree where Clarence lived and, as he neared the tree, he saw Mr. Owl putting his head under his wings, just getting ready for a good day's sleep. Harry hid under some leaves and called out to the owl, 'Excuse me, excuse me please, Mr. Owl.'

'Whooo–whoo, what do you want?' grumbled the owl.

'I'd like to know where I can buy my forty little spiders some new shoes,' asked Harry.

'How can I answer that if I can't see who you are? Now, no nonsense, show your face! Ah ha! Harry Tarantula, no wonder you didn't want me to see you. Lucky for you my tummy is full and I'm ready for bed. Now what is this about shoes?'

Harry timidly explained the situation and Mr. Owl laughed out loud. 'Harry, I'd think that even you would know that insects don't wear shoes. Now go back and tell Tina the truth. That is the silliest idea she's ever had! And do it now, I want to go to sleep!'

Before Harry could get all eight of his legs going, Mr. Owl was already snoring. As Harry was about to leave the forest he heard the owl repeat, 'The truth, Harry, always tell the truth!'

Sure, that's easy for him to say but she'll never believe I talked to an owl and she'll think I said she's silly. What can I do? He thought. I know, I'll tell her that I found the place and they were all sold out and they said for me to come back next year. By then, the kids will all be gone and she will have forgotten all about it. Yeah, that what I'll say! I'd better hurry home before I forget my story.

Harry went running in the front door, ready to tell Tina the story when, what did he see? Forty new spider eggs.

'What on earth?'

'Congratulations, Harry, you're going to be a father again,' said Tina.

Oh, no, thought Harry, it won't do any good to tell her that story now! So, Harry just blurted out the truth to Tina about not being able to find any shoes.

'Harry, my dear. I knew all along insects don't wear shoes. I just needed an excuse to get you out of the house for the day so that after the children left I could get the house cleaned and ready for our new eggs. I knew I could get it done faster if you weren't here,' explained Tina.

'You knew?'

'Yes, you see the black widow told me that's how she gets her spring-cleaning done. But one time, her husband came back and told her the silliest lie about finding the place and that they were sold out until next year. Can you believe anyone would make up a story like that? I'm so proud of you for always telling me the truth,' bragged Tina.

'Yes, I do, don't I?' said Harry proudly.

'What a wise old owl,' he muttered under his breath.

'What did you say?' asked Tina.

'Nothing, just telling the boys and girls goodbye, and reminding them it's always better to tell the truth.'

Andy Rabbit Wants New Skates

'Please, oh, please mommy. Everybody else has them. Why can't I have a pair of skates? Please!' whined Andy.

'Andy, in the first place, everybody else does not have skates. In the second place, we can't afford them; and third, you don't even know how to skate. Besides that, you still haven't learned how to take care of your toys. Do you remember, I said "Nothing else until you learn to put your toys away when you are through playing with them?"' said Momma Rabbit.

'Oh but momma, I will, I promise. I'll wipe them down after I use them and I'll put them back in their box and put them in my closet every time. Oh, please mommy!' begged Andy.

'Andy, I said no. Now that's the end of it. I don't want to discuss this any more,' said momma.

'Gee, momma, that's not fair. You never let me have anything, you're just mean,' pouted Andy.

'Young rabbit, go to your room this minute, and don't

come out until you can apologize.'

Andy stomped off to his room muttering to himself the whole way. 'I wish I was grown, then I'd buy me some skates and I would do whatever I wanted and nobody would ever tell me what to do again. I wish I lived in the forest all by myself. I know what I'll do, I'll run away! Yeah, that's what I'll do, I'll go when everybody is eating supper. They'll be so sorry. Momma will wish she'd been nicer to me.' Andy lay down on his little bed and fell fast asleep.

'Andy wake up, it's time for supper. Go wash your paws. Tell me you're sorry for the way you acted and let's have a nice supper,' said momma as she gently shook Andy awake.

'No, I'm not hungry and I'm not sorry either. Just leave me alone and let me sleep,' said Andy in a not-so-nice tone of voice.

'All right, young rabbit, that's your choice. But you are going to get awfully hungry before breakfast. I hope your attitude changes before morning.' And with that momma walked out, leaving Andy alone in his room.

Andy hurriedly packed his bag and out the window he went, on his way to living all by himself. He scurried along in the tall grass until he reached the forest, and as he came closer, he began to hear all sorts of strange sounds.

Gosh, thought Andy, I don't know what all these noises are. This is kind of spooky and it's getting darker. Golly, I wish I'd eaten some supper before I left. I really need to hurry and find a place to sleep for the night before it gets too dark, and then it'll be too dark to hunt for food. Wonder what momma fixed for supper? Oh dear, what was that? It sounds like an owl. Oh no, it is an owl! I can see it in the sky. Look how big its wings are, and its claws. Oh dear, I've got

to hide, where, where?

Andy ran as fast as a rabbit can go, deeper into the forest. The faster Andy ran, the more scared he became. He dropped his bag, tripped over a log, scraped his knee, but he got back up and ran, crying, farther and farther into the woods.

Finally, Andy came upon an old hollow branch lying on the ground. Yes, thought Andy, at last a safe place to sleep. Andy stopped and listened carefully and he could no longer hear the owl.

Oh, thank you, Jesus, I'll be all right now, he thought. He wiped the tears from his face and crawled into the log. Boy, am I dirty, he thought. Look at all these stickers in my fur. Momma would sure be angry if she could see me eat supper without washing my paws and face. Ha, ha, ha, he thought. Then Andy realized he'd missed supper. His little stomach began to growl. I wish I'd stayed home until after supper, thought Andy. Oh well, I'll find some berries and fruits and grass in the morning. At least I'm safe for the night. I'm so tired, and with that Andy began to doze off to sleep.

★

'Hey! You! Get out of my bed!'

Andy's eyes popped open and his heart was pounding. He was staring into the biggest brown eyes he'd ever seen.

'I said, get out of my bed. If you don't, you're going to be very sorry. I can throw a stink on you like you've never smelled, and if that doesn't work, I may just bite off your head. Young rabbit does taste pretty good.'

Andy jumped up, hitting his head as he scrambled out of

the log. Once again, he was running for his life. He ran until he reached the pond. Thank you, Jesus, there's some water to drink, he thought. I'm thirsty after all this running. Andy dunked his head down into the pond and began to slurp the water. After several big gulps he slowed down, and that's when he heard the voice.

'Water taste good?'

'Why, yes it does!' Andy turned around to greet whomever it was speaking to him and there he was, face to face with a big water snake.

'I wonder,' said the snake, 'if rabbit tastes as good as fish?' The snake uncoiled and started slithering towards Andy. Andy screamed and ran once again as fast as he could, back into the forest.

'Oh, I wish I was back home in my bed!' Andy started to cry softly and he listened to the sounds of the coyotes barking and the bobcats screeching. Maybe if I yell loudly enough my momma will hear me and come find me, he thought, and began to scream at the top of his lungs. 'Momma help me, oh please, momma come find me!'

'Andy, Andy, wake up, Andy. It's momma, you're having a bad dream.'

Andy opened his eyes and there he was at home in his own bed.

'Oh momma, I'm so sorry I was hateful and I don't even want the skates. I just want to be a good little rabbit and never ever leave home,' sobbed Andy.

'Well sweetheart, I guess a good night's sleep did wonders for you, and I hope you and I never have an argument like this again. You see, Andy, it makes mamma rabbits feel just as bad as baby bunnies when they argue. It's really kind of scary to get that mad at someone.'

'Boy, you can say that again!' said Andy as he went over to give his momma a big rabbit hug.